Going to the zoo, cried Miffy Bun

oh yes, that will be great

but it's a long, long way away

I hope the train's not late.

And so they travelled on the train

the proper big train, too

the train ran very very fast

and Miffy watched the view.

They must have travelled for an hour

but now they're there, you see

and Father Bun steps out and says

come Miffy, follow me.

At first they went along a walk

where cheerful parrots sat

the parrots shouted, hello Miff

for parrots talk like that.

And then – what's that? cried Miffy

that funny little horse

a horse with stripes all over it

a zebra? Yes, of course.

They also saw a kangaroo

in front she had a pouch

and that was for her baby roo

as comfy as a couch.

And next they saw an elephant

he's so huge, Miffy said

and look, he's stretching out his trunk

to take a piece of bread.

And have you seen the monkey there

he's swinging on a tree

with just one hand, but monkeys find

it easy, as you see.

Now the giraffes, oh goodness me

their necks are very long

but they won't hurt you, Miffy dear

no, nothing will go wrong.

And when the day was nearly done

now, Miffy, you decide

perhaps the giant tortoise? Yes!

that was a lovely ride.

So everything was over now

the train was standing near

and in the train Miff fell asleep

sleep well now, Miffy dear.

miffy's library

miffy
miffy goes to stay
miffy is crying
miffy's birthday
miffy at school
miffy's bicycle

miffy's dream
miffy at the zoo
miffy in hospital
miffy in the tent
miffy at the seaside
miffy in the snow

miffy goes flying
miffy at the playground
poppy pig
poppy pig is sick
boris on the mountain
boris in the snow

"nijntje in de dierentuin"
Original text Dick Bruna 1988 © copyright Mercis Publishing BV.
Illustrations Dick Bruna © copyright Mercis BV 1988.
Published in Great Britain in 1997 by World International Ltd.,
Deanway Technology Centre, Wilmslow Road, Handforth, Cheshire SK9 3FB.
Original English translation © copyright Patricia Crampton 1996.
Publication licensed by Mercis Publishing BV, Amsterdam.
Printed by Sebald Sachsendruck Plauen, Germany. All rights reserved.
ISBN 0-7498-2986-9

WORLD